AROUND AMERICA
TO WIN THE VOTE

TWO SUFFRAGISTS, A KITTEN,
AND 10,000 MILES

☆ ☆ ☆

MARA ROCKLIFF

illustrated by
HADLEY HOOPER

CANDLEWICK PRESS

On April 6, 1916, a little yellow car set out from New York City.

It carried

tools,

spare parts,

a teeny-tiny typewriter,

an itsy-bitsy sewing machine,

one stout leather trunk bursting with useful things,

two smiling women,

and a wee black kitten with a yellow ribbon tied
    around its neck.

The taller woman was Nell Richardson. The smaller one was Alice Burke. Together, they planned to drive all the way around America. It was a great big country, but they had a great big cause.

"VOTES FOR WOMEN!" Alice told reporters.
"VOTES FOR WOMEN!" Nell agreed.

They said the typewriter and the sewing machine were all part of their plan.

If anyone said women didn't have the brains to vote, then **Nell** would dash a poem off right then and there to prove they *did*.

If anyone said they should cook and sew and leave running the nation to the men, then **Nell** would whip an apron up while Alice gave a speech to prove they could do *both*.

And if the two of them could circle the United States—ten thousand bumpy, muddy, unmapped miles—facing danger and adventure all alone, with just each other (and a kitten) in their little yellow car?

Well, *that* would prove that **WOMEN** could do **ANYTHING.**

So off they went.

That very day, they had their first adventure when a horse pulling a wagon down a narrow road refused to let them pass.

"VOTES FOR WOMEN!" Alice told the horse.

Nell tied a Votes-for-Women-yellow daffodil behind his ear.

Then the horse stepped aside and let the little yellow car go on its way.

In Philadelphia, they stood up on their seats to speak to the great city crowd.

Nell didn't need to write a poem on her typewriter or sew an apron on her sewing machine.

Men and women cheered.

But the next morning . . .

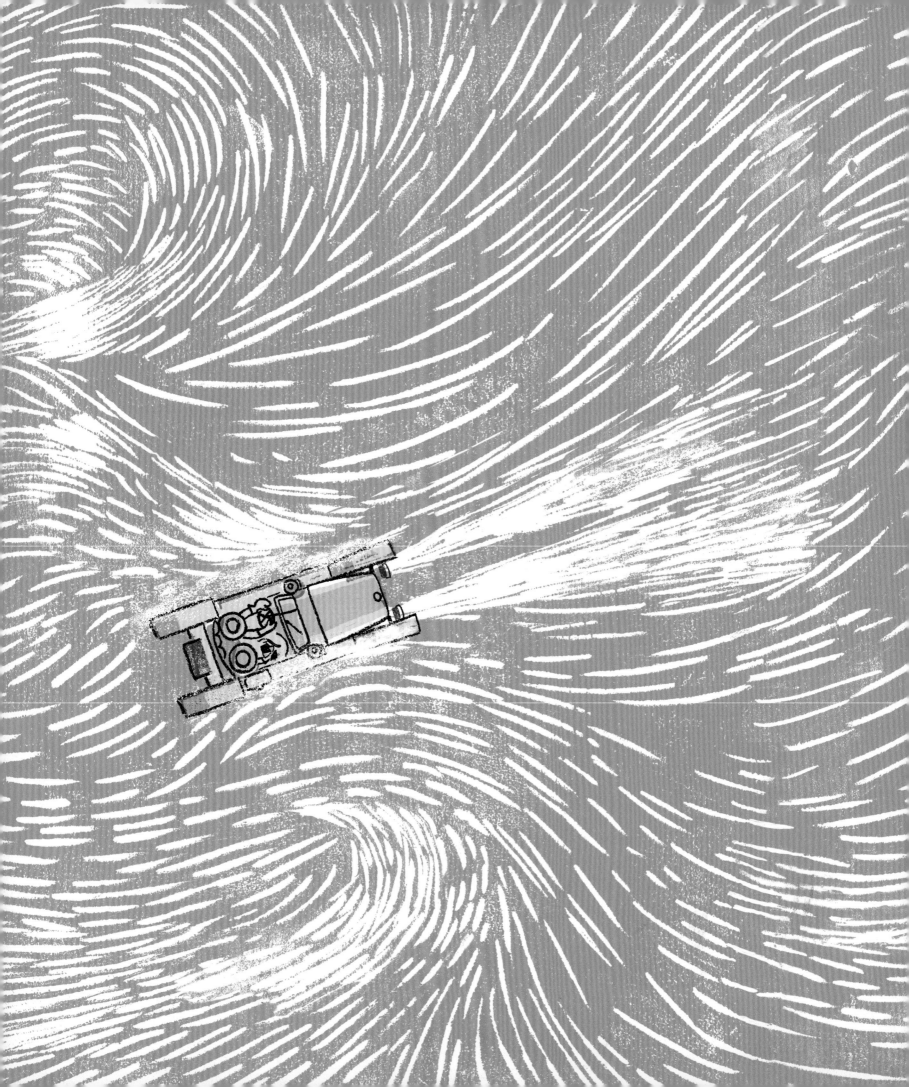

BLIZZARD!
    Nell and **A**lice dug into their trunk of useful things.
    They put on their raincoats and their rubber hats and drove through howling wind and swirling snow to Baltimore . . .

where they arrived
in time to be the
guests of honor at
a very fancy party.
(The trunk held a
few useful things
for parties, too.)

The next day, when they stopped for gas, a crowd of men clustered around the little yellow car.

Alice hopped up on the seat to give her speech.

But no one listened.

So she told them all about the car instead.

"Votes for women!" the men said, and waved as Nell and Alice drove away.

After a quick visit to Washington, D.C., they came upon the bumpiest and muddiest road yet.

The little yellow car went *bump* and *squelch* and finally got stuck.

As the car sank, Nell and Alice jumped into the icy stream. They cranked and cranked and cranked the engine, but it wouldn't start.

"Votes for women!" Nell reminded Alice cheeringly.

Alice grumbled, "And *good roads.*"

In the trunk, they found a lantern
and a blanket and a box of candy from
their friends.

They huddled, wet and shivering, under the blanket
and ate candy till the sun came up and two strong mules
appeared to pull their car out of the mud.

In Virginia, **Nell** and **Alice** passed a school and all the children ran to see the little yellow car.

They hung all over it and wouldn't let the women (or the kitten) go till **Alice** promised to send them a picture postcard from someplace extremely far away.

They drove into
North Carolina,
passing fields
of singing birds
and butterflies
and goldenrod . . .

and nearly fell into a hole where a bridge used to be.

Next came deep puddles . . .

sticky clay . . .

and thick, wet sand.

In South Carolina, a whole town turned out and treated them to an all-yellow lunch.

In Georgia, they joined a circus parade.

In **Alabama**, the two travelers sipped tea and nibbled on stuffed dates.

Everywhere, they met crowds.
Everywhere, Nell and Alice told them: "V. for W.!"

Outside Gulfport, Mississippi,
the little yellow car finally found
a mud puddle it couldn't cross.
They sneaked the kitten
onto the train . . .

and smuggled it into a fine hotel in **New Orleans**.

Then the little car arrived, and they were on their way.

They dodged bullets by the Rio Grande . . .

drove on through
the desert of
New Mexico . . .

and got lost for days
in **Arizona** . . .

till, finally, they reached . . .

CALIFORNIA!
Where they won a medal at the fair for driving a long way to get there—all the way across America.

But they were only halfway to the finish line. They still had lots of miles and lots of adventures on the road ahead.

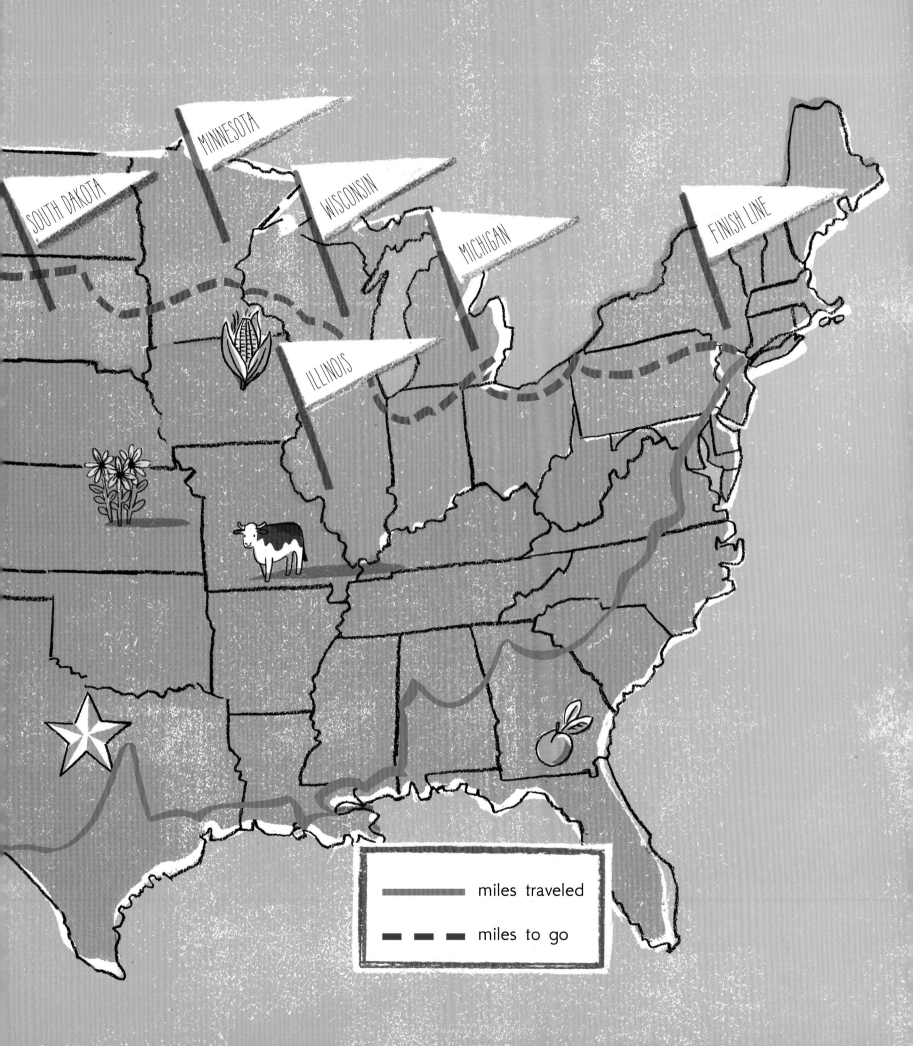

On September 30, 1916, a little yellow car drove into New York City.

It carried mud and dust and signatures and souvenirs from all around America, two smiling (and sunburned) women, and a full-grown cat.

They arrived to a grand welcome . . .

and a great big yellow cake.
    (The cat ate seven slices,
as reported in the next
morning's *Tribune*.)

After ten thousand bumpy, muddy, unmapped miles,
Nell was ready for a rest.

And Alice?
She turned right around and crossed the country all
over again.

This time, she took the train.

THAT NEWFANGLED MACHINE!

In the early 1900s, only the very adventurous would even try to drive across America. The first to succeed was a Vermont doctor named H. Nelson Jackson, who drove from California to New York in 1903. Six years later, Alice Ramsey of New Jersey became the first woman to finish the cross-country trip. Neither of them traveled half as far as Alice Burke and Nell Richardson would in 1916, driving all day and making public speeches every night.

By 1916, automobiles had become quite popular, but driving was still a challenge. Gas stations weren't common yet, so Nell and Alice would have stopped at country stores or farms to fill their tank. Instead of road maps, they had to rely on the "Blue Book," which gave directions like "Turn right at the yellow barn"—not so helpful if the barn had fallen down or been repainted red!

Nell and Alice drove a little "runabout" made by the Saxon Motor Car Company. They called it the Golden Flier. Before they left New York, it was officially christened by suffrage leader Carrie Chapman Catt, using a champagne bottle filled with gasoline. Newspapers reported that Catt brought the bottle down so hard, she left the radiator with a dent.

Alice also called the car their "yellow baby" and bragged about how well it ran. "The little baby motor car has been true to us," she wrote. "We can't blame her when she gets stuck in the mud." They even named the kitten Saxon. In turn, the Saxon Company used Nell and Alice in an ad. Like many ads, it stretched the truth, claiming that the two travelers sped easily from one place to the next and "were never late once."

Yesterday we went up slowly toward a white mule that was drawing a long wagon, and he seemed perfectly serene, when suddenly he turned to his right and jumped wildly over a five-foot embankment. For an instant we had a vision of the old white mule with his ears laid back flat, his tail flying out straight behind, and a long, thin wagon in the air. . . . Then mule, wagon, and driver struck ground right side up, and with no damage done except to the King's English, which suffered a bit when the driver told the mule just what he thought of him.

Alice S. Burke, "Diary of the Golden Flier,"
Boston Globe, April 22, 1916

WINNING THE VOTE

Alice and Nell's journey may sound long and hard, but it was quick and easy compared to the journey American women undertook to win the vote.

In 1776, future First Lady Abigail Adams wrote to her revolutionary husband, John, urging him to "Remember the ladies." She said that if American men were willing to fight for independence and a say in their own government, so were American women. John Adams wrote back, "I cannot but laugh." Soon after, he signed the Declaration of Independence, which stated that "all men are created equal." Women were left out.

In 1848, a group of women including Elizabeth Cady Stanton and Lucretia Mott held a meeting at Seneca Falls, New York. There, they signed their own declaration, stating that "all men and women are created equal." But to make women equal under the law, they knew they had to win the right to vote.

Seventy-two years had passed since Abigail Adams spoke up for women's rights. It would take exactly seventy-two more to reach her goal.

The women—and some men—who fought this battle were called suffragists. (*Suffrage* means the right to vote.) Along with Mott and Stanton, they included leaders such as Lucy Stone, Susan B. Anthony, Sojourner Truth, Alice Paul, and Ida B. Wells. They also included hundreds of thousands of lesser-known heroes like Nell Richardson and Alice Burke.

These women defied husbands and fathers to march in the streets and make speeches. (Every night for six months, Alice stood on a wooden soapbox at the corner of Broadway and 96th Street in New York City, cheerfully haranguing passersby.)

As the years went by, the suffragists got creative. They wrote songs. They drew cartoons. One pilot suffragist "bombed" carnival crowds with leaflets from a plane. Another, hoping to reach coal miners, wore overalls and went down 2,500 feet below the ground. Suffragists even made the Statue of Liberty speak. The words that came out of its mouth, of course, were "Votes for Women."

The year 1916 was an exciting one. Jeannette Rankin of Montana—one of the eleven western states where women had the vote—became the first woman elected to Congress. It was an election year for the president of the United States as well, and suffragists planned huge demonstrations to persuade both sides to give women the vote. At the Republican convention in Chicago, thousands of women and girls marched in the freezing rain behind a baby elephant draped in a rubber blanket that said "Votes for Women." The next week, in St. Louis, they held a "walkless parade." Men on their way to the Democratic convention had to pass between eight thousand silent suffragists lining the streets for a mile on both sides.

These demonstrators came from all over the country. Many must have heard about the plans from Nell and Alice, who used their cross-country trip to spread the word. At the time of the conventions, the pair had just arrived in California. But they didn't stop. They knew their work was not yet done.

The next year, the United States entered World War I. Many suffragists set aside their own goals to help with the war effort. Others, led by Alice Paul, kept up the fight. They picketed the White House, asking Woodrow Wilson why democracy abroad was more important than democracy at home. Mobs attacked the peaceful protesters while police stood by and watched. Then the police began arresting suffragists, who hadn't broken any law. In prison, the women were treated so badly—and resisted so bravely—that public opinion turned. Americans demanded votes for women *now*.

In 1920, the Nineteenth Amendment was officially added to the U.S. Constitution. It states, "The right of citizens of the United States to vote shall not be denied or abridged by the United States or by any State on account of sex."

At last, American women had won the right to vote.

A NOTE ON SOURCES

Two women (and a kitten) driving ten thousand miles to win the vote? In 1916, that was news, and newspapers around America followed their trip. Using hundreds of old articles, including three written by Alice Burke herself, I was able to piece the story together. Everything that happens in this book comes from news accounts of the time.

Of course, even newspapers can make mistakes. For instance, several claimed that Nell and Alice had visited every state in the union other than the six New England states. Mapping out their journey using every town and city where I could be sure they stopped, I quickly realized that wasn't true. Instead, they'd made a giant loop around the country, skipping North Dakota, Florida, and all the "middle" states.

A number of my sources came to me from independent researcher and automobile enthusiast Jeryl Schriever. Without her, I would have missed important parts of this forgotten story. I'd like to thank Jeryl and her husband, Alex Huppé, who not only patiently answered my many questions, but even let me drive a real Baby Saxon, just like Nell and Alice's!

I'd also like to thank Patri O'Gan, whose blog post for the National Museum of American History introduced me to Alice and Nell (and, of course, the kitten).

WHY ALL THE YELLOW?

The color yellow stood for Votes for Women everywhere in the United States.

FOR FURTHER READING

Brown, Don. *Alice Ramsey's Grand Adventure.* Boston: Houghton Mifflin, 1997.

Kamma, Anne. *If You Lived When Women Won Their Rights.* Illustrated by Pamela Johnson. New York: Scholastic, 2008.

Koehler-Pentacoff, Elizabeth. *Jackson and Bud's Bumpy Ride: America's First Cross-Country Automobile Trip.* Illustrated by Wes Hargis. Minneapolis: Millbrook, 2009.

MacDonald, Fiona. *You Wouldn't Want to Be a Suffragist! A Protest Movement That's Rougher Than You Expected.* Illustrated by David Antram. New York: Franklin Watts, 2008.

Rappaport, Doreen. *Elizabeth Started All the Trouble.* Illustrated by Matt Faulkner. New York: Disney-Hyperion, 2016.

Stone, Tanya Lee. *Elizabeth Leads the Way: Elizabeth Cady Stanton and the Right to Vote.* Illustrated by Rebecca Gibbon. New York: Henry Holt, 2008.

White, Linda Arms. *I Could Do That! Esther Morris Gets Women the Vote.* Illustrated by Nancy Carpenter. New York: Farrar, Straus and Giroux, 2005.

For Roseanne and Rob, who always go
that extra mile (or ten thousand)
M. R.

For Dash, who was born ninety-five years to the day
after women got the right to vote
H. H.

Text copyright © 2016 by Mara Rockliff
Illustrations copyright © 2016 by Hadley Hooper

First edition 2016

Library of Congress Catalog Card Number 2015940254
ISBN 978-0-7636-7893-7

16 17 18 19 20 21 CCP 10 9 8 7 6 5 4 3 2 1

Printed in Shenzhen, Guangdong, China

This book was typeset in GFS Neohellenic.
The illustrations were done in pencil and printmaking techniques,
then scanned and completed digitally.

Candlewick Press
99 Dover Street
Somerville, Massachusetts 02144

visit us at www.candlewick.com